Olympus Heights

by

Kevin Carey and Colleen Michaels

LILY POETRY REVIEW BOOKS

Table of Contents

Olympus Heights

Truly elevated living. This mountain-side gated community looks over the valley and the ocean and the small humans below. Views of snow-capped peaks from every home. A short drive to the shore. Golf. Tennis. Spa. Houses built for your ego. Secure. Elegant. Immaculate. You know who you are. You deserve this. You're in gods' country.

THE GATES SPEAKS

Given to fault/lines in the sand
built on backs/of melted shields
I'm a hype man/a common folly
rest assured/my rust belt fumes
run this place/of gods and men
my slag has been/separated out
the spreading part/of me I miss.

Pre-construction. Gaia Privatizes Tartarus

For the mortals in the valley

The formula is simple: If it fills,
build another one. And the laws?
They're as flexible as prosecutorial misconduct.
Nothing like the threat of a deep,
dark abyss to keep the order.
I'm less interested in Eros.
What's the fun with love
when punishment is an option:
Take a name in vain,
forget the sacrifice,
utter the wrong word within
earshot. Whatever it takes
to pack the pens, keep the gates
opening and closing. Afterall,
the only cure for chaos is system.

Cronus On a Group Chat With His Sister
and The Kids

Annoyed. They are all
hard to swallow, even Zeus,
who makes him throw up.

Hera Shops at Whole Foods to Feel Alive

Contemplating the self-serve
soap bar, she dreams of a clean kill.

Here, you are allowed to cut your own
so she portions herself a sliver

lemon verbena, sometimes charcoal
and tobacco, cruelty-free promises.

She pockets the sickle moon, struts
peacock style to the dairy and non-dairy aisle

where with one side eye she besets a constellation
of allergies from nut milks to new mothers.

It is no coincidence that *Echo and the Bunnymen*
is in heavy rotation on her shopping days. Humming

about fate and killing, her nail pierces the flesh
of a pomegranate and then an apple.

She returns the produce cut side down to bleed or bruise
then scrawls on a comment card: "Pawed fruit. Do better."

When the cashier asks, *Prime Member?* She hears *Prime Number*
and responds. *Yes. Don't dare try to put me in a line with others.*

Zeus on Instagram

Big Z
a bird's eye view of a stone mansion on a hill,
other homes neatly laid out on a grid below,
folks mowing lawns, kids riding bikes.

Comment: *Made it ma, top of the world.*

Big Z
a tall broad bearded man in a new dark suit
a few other men from the neighborhood lying
unconscious at his feet.

Comment: *I've crushed more revolts than Castro.*

Big Z
a tall blonde in a red bikini stepping
out of a pool

Comment: *Happy Anniversary Hera / C U Next Tuesday*

Big Z
a bull, a cuckoo, and a swan posing in
a mid-century canopy bed

Comment: *Still crazy spreading the seed.*

Big Z
the front yard of a stone mansion
hundreds of people crammed into the frame.

Comment: *Fathers Day with the youngins*

Origin Story: Hestia, First Born

The last spit out and the first to be born
is bringing a hammer to a gunfight.
Every household needs a martyr to mourn,

so I take the obstructed view, am sworn
to keep the peace on holiday nights
when they spit out orders to me, firstborn.

My brother the drunk, all siblings inborn
with a meanness that cankers like peach blight.
Every household needs a martyr. To mourn

my siblings, to trade bud for thorn,
to throw a punch, set fires all night,
be the last word spit. Not the first thought born.

I bring the casseroles heavy and warm.
Be the change, in my grace journal I write
Hold onto your house. Need a martyr to mourn?

Choose me! The virgin, a rare unicorn,
who never played musical chairs quite right.
The last spit out and the first to be born,
every household needs a martyr to mourn.

Hades, The Man Next Door

Cerberus shits on the new green lawn by the mulched flower bed. *Good boys.* My brother tells me I should pick it up, *be a good neighbor,* he says. I tell him he's all wet. Today his wife looks out the kitchen window, holds up a poop bag and smiles. *Does she smell Minthe on me?* In the Greek Revival across the street I see my brother's kid (don't ever live near family). He mouths *Pluto* from behind the glass slider. *One eyed dimwit.* Maybe I'll take him to the basement one day, cover him with a pile of fighting men slain in cruel wars. Watch him eat his way out. He'll know when I'm coming for him. *Not such a good trade after all, Bug Eye.*

Spring Break Persephone

My mother won't stop texting,
doesn't know I can see her

ellipsis hovering, and feel
her wanting.

How was your day? School alright?
I don't tell her I dyed my hair

black and inked my inner
wrist with a semicolon

that I'll rework into a red petal.
A freshman, unfinished

just wants a mother who gardens
in a plot further away,

wants her need to melt like ice
in a red solo cup.

Daughters will go down to Hades.
Mothers will search to the ends

with a torch in hand that can
burn a field between them.

The tether now slack
on Persephone's end of the line

she's not coming home
for winter or spring break.

Demeter: Still Touchy After All These Years

She feeds on revenge
like fodder
if you don't believe me
just mess with her daughter

Remind her of Hades
then head for the door
she'll lay waste to the soil
the whole threshing-floor

Best not piss her off
but give what she needs
choose wisely my friend
no pomegranate seeds.

Otitis Externa: Poseidon Refuses Treatment for Swimmer's Ear

Children won't listen and try to make a whirlpool the first time
they visit someone else's inground. Legs like colts cutting the wrong
direction through pristine chlorine. It's a form of pissing. My sons
are better swimmers than my brothers' kids. Part fish, they high dive,
butterfly. They medal, then high five. Marco….Polo. Soon they will
arrive at a grotto like Hefner's - I'll take them there - young and slick
dolphins, wearing puka necklaces and bragging about a boat that does
not yet belong to them. My boat. My cigarette boat, fast and loud.
Like a leaf blower on a Saturday, in my brother's neighborhood (the
brother who can rot in Hell). But, so much cooler. Sex is a form of
waterboarding, I tell my boys. Don't let up. Go long. It's a swimming
contest. I met their mothers in the summers of blockbuster disaster
movies. I divorced the ones who closed their eyes during tsunami
scenes. Tried to keep the ones who got off on cruise ships sinking.
Some I asked to hold their breath underwater, and waved goodbye to
the ones who could beat my time, the ones I caught wincing when I
asked them to slather my back with sunscreen, the ones who made a
horsey noise and ate all the celery from my bloody marys. The ones
who thought the privilege of a glass bottle on the pool deck was theirs
and theirs alone. The ones who refused to pick up my towels. The ones
who would cannonball near my best chair.

Boreas Chills at the Pool Party

standing by the pool shed, alone,
shaggy hair and a billowing cloak
over his wings,
a half-smoked joint in his lips.
A whisper. "Who invited him?"
He knows what they think –
lesser god. He hears the gossip
over the Hip Hop. "That dude is cold."
He knows they won't warm up to him,
didn't even get an invite,
just blew in from Thrake mountains like a snow squall.
Another snicker – "It's August for fuck's sake."
After the home grown kicks in, he's a little
closer, eyeing the party like *Aqualung*
at the playground, his icy breath freezing
the deep end by the slide.

Artemis Drafts a Memo of Understanding
to the Homeowners' Association

"Here is the problem with encountering a deity: if you're not ready, you're going to make a mistake and get blown to pieces."

Joseph Campbell describing Artemis

Pursuant to parking guidelines:

        The boss hog stays on the lawn.

Regarding home occupancy limits:

        My moon is exclusive and open.
        The occupancy of my bedroom is a non-starter.

Noise complaint policy rider:

        Baying in labor, a howl or growl.
        Fine. Fine. Fine.

Policy on packages and deliveries:

        I'll grant safe passage to Amazon women only,
        their quivers delivered under my porch slats.

Home maintenance standards:

        Dartboards are now mandatory in every garage.

Limits on pet size and quantity:

        My yard remains waist-deep in Irish Wolfhounds.
        In heat. In perpetuity.

Lawn decoration restriction amendment:

        The display of my taxidermy is my sticking point.
        I have painted the eyes historical hunter green.

JP Morgan Tells Apollo He's Too Big to Fail

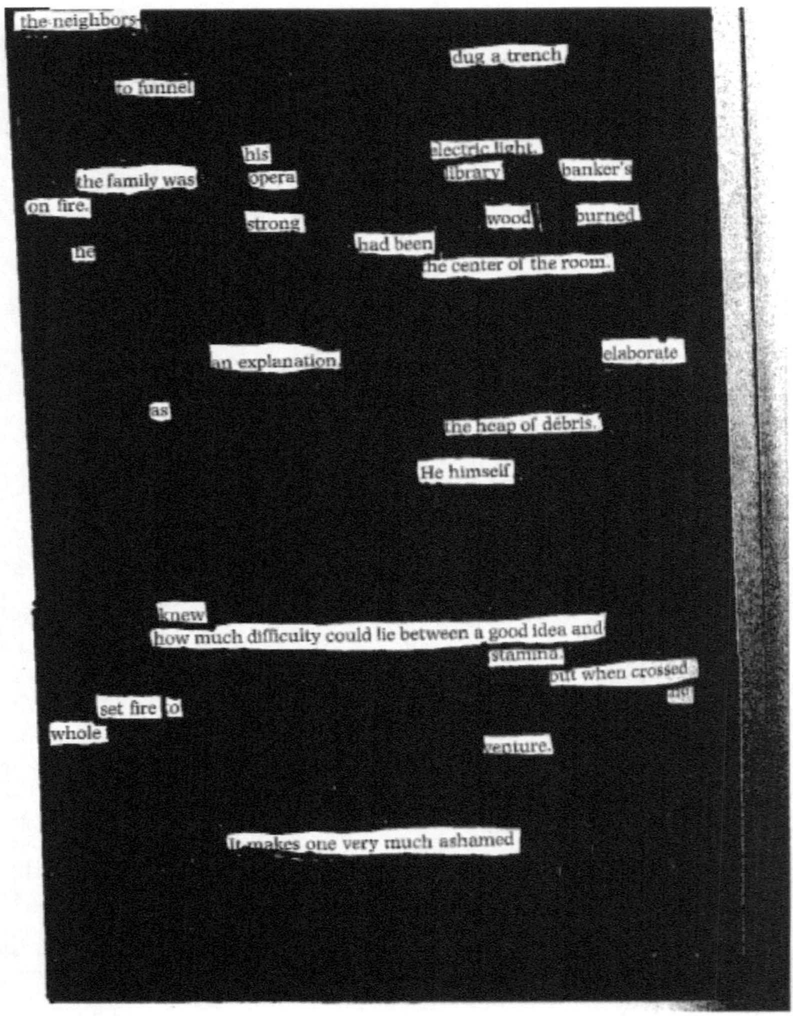

Iris Insists on Installing Solar Panels

She leaves on the weekends to go god
knows where, flea markets, crystal shopping
she's a Greek comedy, always extra, pushing
some cheerful free tote bag.

I heard both her kids are gay. No, I didn't bring
it up to the Board. What could I say? They
saw her rainbow flag, a violation for sure.
I just want you to know. She's spreading

her flyers on the community board again
getting estimates for that ugly light, will stop
you in your tracks to talk and talk
until you burn red, until you ignite.

Hephaestus Remembers the War Lobbyists

They ask me: *Hephaestus, what'd you want: golf junkets, Caribbean
cruises, young girls from Serbia?* I keep them in the shields. Pour gold
for the righteous fights. They all want one like Achilles, the story on
the sleeve. The children on my street chant *Hey smithy you're so ugly*
but that won't stop me from dropping my seed, hammering myself
into every god-fueled battle. I ain't no looker, but all the big shots
come to me because they know I pound that anvil day and night.
Keep the machine rolling. War's the ticket and bling's the thing.
Chant all you want pretty little ones. Who do you think made
Achilles a star? Swords, shields, breast plates you want 'em I got 'em,
even a golden chair for the right lady, strings attached.

Police Log #1: Midnight. Saturday, the 30th ####.
Officers called to Olympus Heights. Complaints of
loud cries and thunder bolts

At the gates, the sound of goblets breaking, a man stares at himself
in a pool with a gun raised to his head, just as another rolls through
the square strapped to a giant fire wheel. Human sized spiders hang
by the neck from a gutter. One drunken centaur chases frogs before
a lion attacks. A few stoned elders stare lifeless at the scene. A young
man wanders about braying, "I have donkey ears." He does. A pack of
wild dogs maul a stag, and one man-child makes a meal of himself on
a banquet table. Pockets of limbless bodies, a flayed corpse, and a head
sliced at the neck on a nearby front lawn. One white heifer eats grass.
A turtle looks on from a pool-side lounge.

Ares, God of Violence, Shops for New Clothes

He has a hole but not the inclination to mend himself.
There is a seamstress, let's call her Hope, who works part time
at a department store at the Mall of America, so he brings her his suit.
Wants to show off. *Look how I've burst at the seams.*
She holds the pins in her mouth. Again deals with a man and his arms.
Knowing that even on her knees, at the hem of violence, she is working
to shape a better silhouette. It takes some doing. Ares is enormous.

Violence is not so different from fast fashion. We hate it and we buy it.
Poor Hope, who's on the way out, drafts patterns to fit what we
openly wear or choose to conceal. Our bodies expect a poor fit.
It's no surprise that Ares never picked up the altered suit.
Who has the patience? The time? He lost the claim ticket. He'll claim
it was not his loss. Ask him about his wardrobe of armor. He'll tell you
he gave up on fixing the hole, tried to grab anything off of the rack to cover
himself, but it was easier, way more fun, to buy another gun.

Moros Applies for a Job at Starbucks

Full name?

Personification of Destiny.

For real?

Or Doom.

Let's go with that. Easier on the name tag. Experience?

Most folks like to ignore me -- to keep bad things from happening to them.

We can keep you in the back. Any criminal record?

Some misfortune and some suffering, small stuff.

Have you worked in a restaurant before?

No but sometimes I can turn invisible.

No shit? Can you work nights? Weekends?

If it's meant to be.

Any history of allergies, triggers, abuse, addiction, traumas, aban-

donment, phobias, nightmares, middle-school scars, bad breakups,

emotional pit falls, crying spells, disorientation, fatigue, brain fog or

irrational fears?

I was once afraid Zeus would kill me.

Did he try?

No. He knows that chaos would reign.

That's a paradox.

You tell me.

I just did. Tomorrow okay to start?

Sounds like the plan.

Origin Story: Athena After Being Told
She's Her Father's Daughter

He never admits I got my brains from my mother,
says she's the high-pitched hiss of a fridge
on the fritz, but I feel her at my shoulder.

She sews an owl into my collar, blocks
the view of his gun display case on prom night. She knows
we're all going together as a group anyway. She gets me.

My father is a voracious eater. Sends my mother out of the room
before he tells his stories to his students, all spinning plates
and passing cigars, the students he forces to come to Sunday dinner.

The school spelling bee, crescent moons under my arms and armor,
the heat of the auditorium lights, I hear *Anima* but maybe *Animus*.
I want a definition of *Us*. Ask for clarification. I want her. *Counsel.*

During my debate society's winning rebuttal, my father
strains from his balcony seat, yelling, *she gets it from me!*
Sometimes pride is a boa constrictor at the neck.

We don't stop at the Dairy Queen on the way home,
see the runners up on the benches
with their mothers, the consolations in their mouths.

Hermes's Garage

Not exactly a hoarder, and not exactly a surprise,
his body was discovered beside the stolen belongings.
Carrier of petty grievances, a bookie, the fence between
neighbors. Always liked to play CLUE. And he did
that little thing when he was telling a story. *I know this guy*
you see. Spoiler: He's always the guy. God of quick-to-tire-of
was always around somehow, fastest to the doorbell.
It was Poseidon. In the deep end. With your wife.
Bada Bing. Wocka Wocka. Everyone hated the sounds
he made around a joke. *Did you hear that? Your wife.*
We couldn't get past the track suit, the golf cart,
the mortal, mortal breath, the close talking, the one
liners that fell like backward footsteps. He'd hover
in the sales office, giving prospective buyers his take,
leading poor souls on hellish tours of the compost
bins and saying "all eyes on me" in that needy high-
pitched voice. He died with his glory days pinned
to his sharkskin suit, he died by falling off a truck.
He died fast. The quick and the dead. Bada Bing. He
dropped like a mercury balloon. Wocka Wocka. No will.
He died in wingtip shoes. More mortal than most, he died.

My Neighbor, My Nemesis

My new shovel, you "borrowed"
rusts on your porch.
It's April. Indignation
makes a gully
between our property
as I pray the slant in
your direction. How can you
not own your own sump pump?

I bought a lace leaf house plant
a raw tongue and pointing finger. A comfort.
I gooseneck to catch you
stooping to scoop shit.
I want you to see me,
seeing you
bend low.

Aphrodite Updates Her Tinder Profile

The snap you see is only of my lips, *Runway Red,* slightly parted. I know what you're thinking! I'm not just all brains. I'm popular in the neighborhood for *sho.* I can be a bit of a motherfu…(watch my mouth!). You won't be sorry if you swipe my way. I'll roll up on you like sea foam on the beach, you'll crash all the best parties, and I'm sweet as a dove.

Pros:

I'm hot (for real). Just ask Paris.
My tears make babies.
I won't kiss and tell (and you better not, lol)

Cons:

I've been around. It only makes me better.
I've been known to curse.
You might bleed to death in my arms (just kidding, not)

Bellerophon Bellies Up to the Bar

Something strong. Long week. Went to see a man about a horse, woke up in the wrong temple, got accused of rape. It doesn't end there. Hit me again, will ya? There's a beef with the Amazons and some Carian pirate on my ass. And the final straw: The old man rings me. Tells me to get the lead out. I tell him what I know, right? The lead is buried in a fire breathing goat. So I fly up there for a greet and he makes me lug these thunderbolts around all day. So, no I'm not leaving them outside. Do I look like a gadfly? I asked him. That didn't go over. Shit, I got tossed from a horse with wings, you don't see me blubbering in my beer, do you? Keep em coming. I'll drink till I'm blind.

Dionysus Throws a Wine Tasting

tables covered in silk cloth,
crystal goblets around
the moist mounds of grapes,
a string quartet by the fire pit
everyone nodding appreciation
like an obedient vine cult.
It gets a bit blurry after that
some goblets smashing
wine dribbling off my chin
someone's ass in my hand
the three daughters of Minyas
groping in a pile by the pool
the Amazon Queens chanting
he so divine with all his wine,
neighbors pawing each other,
me yelling *fuck you all*
the cheese floating in a Cabernet
the one-eyed dolt yelling
Chug it and Hera
raising her glass
Your grandma's not around to
put you back together
something sharp in my hand,
some screams, wine flowing
to the patio, and blood
a thunder crack maybe
then the morning light,
and I'm draped
over a lounge chair,
a few bodies by the pool barely
moving, a broken violin at my feet,
my head, the size of a medicine
ball and Staphylus standing over me,
Dad you've got to stop drinking.

Achilles Was a First Round Pick

Now the star sits at home, still the coolest
house on the street, floor to ceiling
windows, an infinity pool,
polished trophies,
game jerseys, basketballs in glass cases.

Most nights he sits in the dark
watching old game films
like Gloria Swanson and her silent movies.
He's put on weight, drinks too much wine,
and blames Thetis (they don't talk anymore).
When asked about it he says, *she didn't
finish the job. Not a closer.*

But back in the day he was *Buckets.*
Thetis in the stands for every game
wearing his jersey
and the jewelry he
bought for her after his
max deal.

Now who's not good enough (Zeus)
she chimed, *check out the bling.*
She was a proud mama, front row
with all the Nerieds fawning over her—
your boy is the greatest.
I know, she'd say. *I made him.*

They took up an entire section
the league's biggest posse.
Achilles beat down Hector's team
time after time. 40 one night, 30 the next,
double digit rebounds, game-winning threes.

I've seen this movie before,
he sniped to the defeated warrior
on his way off the court, *and I win every time.*
The playoffs were in the bag,
they said. No one could stay with Achilles,
it's like he was a god. But that cheat Paris,
one dirty play and a career-ending injury:
Achille's heel crushed like chalk.

Heracles Mans the Guard Shack

Give me that little wave
and I'll let you pass.
I'm not that guy you think,
the murderer husband,
the half-breed cattle poacher.
I'm one of the twelve now
(so the old man says).
My bronze-armored shoulders
crammed into this square hole, no AC,
no lions or hydras or Stymphalian Birds
to wrap my mitts around.
Just Amazon delivery trucks,
golfers, folks in tennis whites,
passing through and smiling
at the neighborhood watchman,
everyone's bodyguard,
the once-was grid-iron champ,
girdle-stealer, bear-hugger,
breath-taker, squeezing
two dead garden snakes
like the old days.

Police Log #2: A demigod cited for driving
to endanger when his chariot crashed through the
Olympus Heights gates and damaged
a police cruiser

Officers took the reins away and told him to walk home.

Amenities: A Common Green
with Life-Sized Chessboard

The underside of hosta is the shade of old money, a garden
juiced by the stars. Orchard of golden apples borders the field

where weeds are the mortal enemy. We've put in a fire pit that sparks
like gossip spitting. Here, we can be off leash and monstrous.

The poor rooked humans, lined up by class on engineered grass. Plastic
so easy to place or replace, we don't worry about rainy days.

We love to rally around our green and play a closed-loop weekend match.
Horseshoes and luck are for chumps. We prefer the immortal game.

Our statuary and topiary find the kings and queens laughable
in their earnest pursuit, their gambit, the funny little game of skill.

On Thursdays we let the pawns fish in the deep reflecting pool.
To keep them happy, we feed them the lie that the pond is stocked daily.

The staff tends to arrows strewn at horses and bishops in toppled golf carts.
We like to play with humans. Set them up. Move them about.

Notes:

The underlying text for "J.P. Morgan Tells Apollo He's Too Big to Fail" comes from page 234 of *Morgan: American Financier* by Jean Strouse (Random House, 2014).

Acknowledgements:

Mom Egg Review: "Hera Shops at Wholefoods to Feel Alive."

Santa Fe literary Review: "Origin Story: Athena After Being Told She's Her Father's Daughter."

WhimsicalPoet: A Journal of Contemporary Poetry. "Achilles Was a First Round Pick."

About the Authors

Kevin Carey is Coordinator of Creative Writing at Salem State University. Books include: *The Beach People (2014)*, *The One Fifteen to Penn Station (2012)*, *Jesus Was a Homeboy (2016)* which was an Honor book for the Paterson Literary Prize, *& Set in Stone (2020)*. His poems have appeared on *The Writers Almanac on National Public Radio* three times and on *The Academy of American Poets Poem a Day*. Kevin is also a playwright and a filmmaker. He has co-directed & co-produced two documentaries about poets, *All That Lies Between Us* and *Unburying Malcolm Miller*. A crime novel, *Murder in the Marsh*, from Darkstroke Books, was released in October (2020). A new middle grade novel *Junior Miles and the Junkman* dropped in September of 2023 from Fitzroy Books / Regal House Publishing. Kevin is the co-founder of *Molecule: a tiny lit mag*. Kevincareywriter.com

Colleen Michaels is the author of *Prize Wheel* (Small Bites Press, 2023) and the editor of *Salem Power: Poems from the 2014 Improbable Places Poetry Tour* (Derby Wharf Light Box, 2023). Her poems have appeared in journals and anthologies including *Passages North, Nixes Mate, The Paterson Literary Review, Cider Press Review, Barrelhouse, Modern Grimoire: Contemporary Fairy Tales, Fables and Folklore* (Indigo Ink Press), and *Raising Lilly Ledbetter: Women Poets Occupy the Work Space* (Lost Horse Press). Her poems have been commissioned as installations for The Massachusetts Poetry Festival, The Peabody Essex Museum, and The Trustees of Reservations. She directs the Writing Studio at Montserrat College of Art in Beverly, Massachusetts, where she began the Improbable Places Poetry Tour, bringing poetry to unlikely places like tattoo parlors, laundromats, and swimming pools. Yes, in the swimming pool. Colleenmichaels.com